Then he saved their lives, and
they swore never to leave him.

We give you
the Secret-Hairy-
Snot-Tooth Oath
of Devotion.

We're
awesome!

And
fun!

And
SCARY!

Are we
scary? I'm
not sure I'm
very scary.

One thing was certain –
Billy's life would never be
the same **AGAIN**...

Contents

Chapter 1
Miserable Mondays
5

Chapter 2
Into the Pool
22

Chapter 3
Overboard!
34

Chapter 4
The Competition
46

Chapter 5
Champion!
62

Chapter 6
Monster Gala
74

Chapter 1
Miserable Mondays

Billy was feeling fed up. It was Monday and that meant swimming lessons.

Mondays are miserable.

Billy **HATED** swimming lessons.

The Mini Monsters were doing everything they could to cheer him up.

Gloop did his eyeball trick.

Ta da!

Captain Snott sang his favourite song.

Happy Snottday to you, Happy Snottday to you...

Trumpet offered Billy a piece of (slightly mouldy) cheese.

But nothing seemed to work.

Swimming isn't that bad, is it?

"I don't like the way the water goes **up my nose.**"

"And down my ears," said Billy.

"Or the way my hair always gets stuck in my swimming hat."

"But worst of all, I'm **TERRIBLE** at it. Last week, Mr. Roberts said I swam like a mad monkey."

"And today there's going to be a diving competition. All the mums and dads are coming. But I can't

j
U
m
P

off a diving board."

"Why don't we come too?" said Captain Snott.

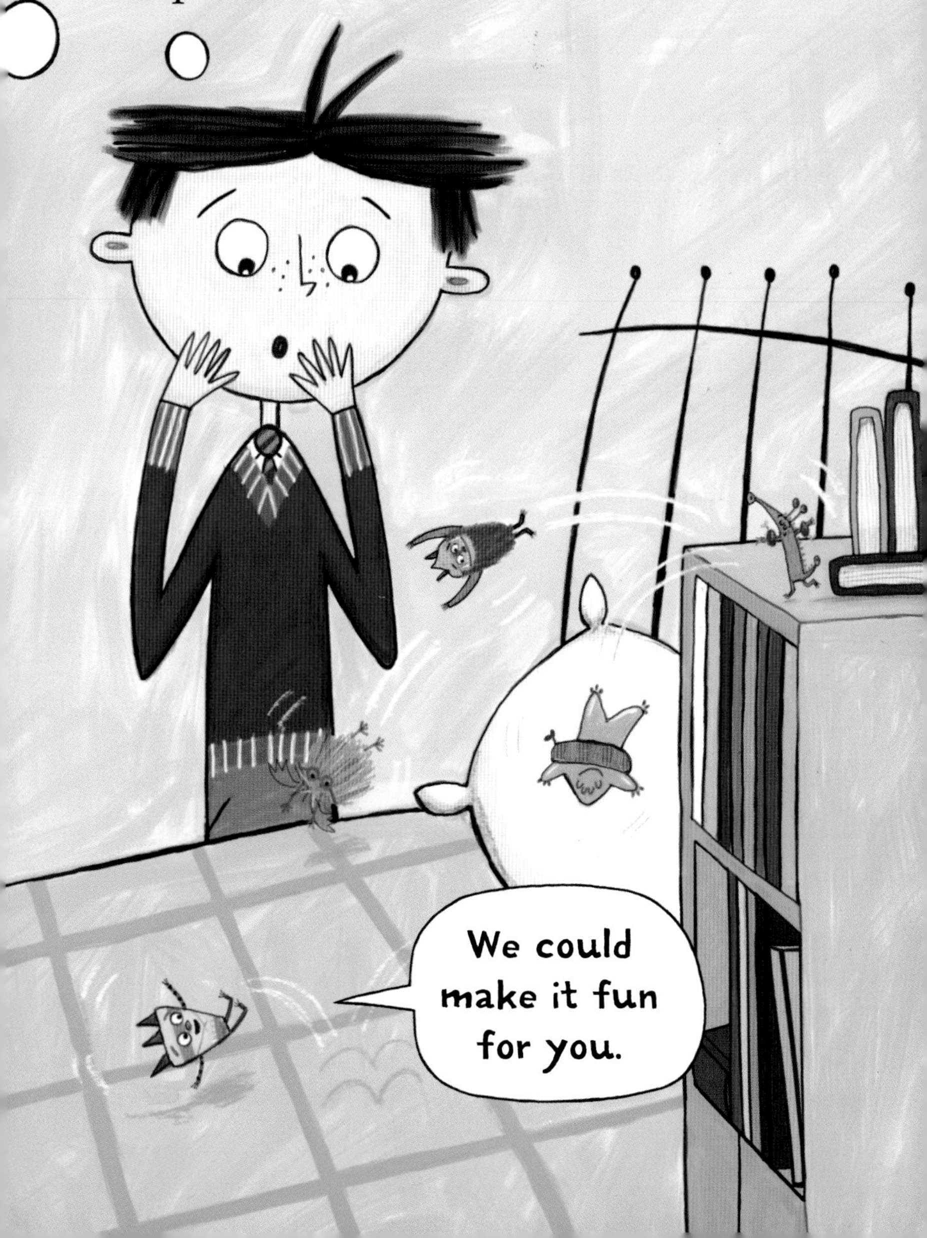

"No way!" said Billy. "That would be a **DISASTER**."

The Mini Monsters were ALWAYS getting into trouble. Billy could just imagine what would happen if they came to the pool…

Gloop being sucked down a drain.

Where am I?

Peep getting lost in the lockers.

Captain Snott showing off.

Fang-Face getting stuck.

Trumpet disappearing on a cheese hunt.

Cheese!

13

"What I need," said Billy, "is a plan to get out of swimming."

PLAN TO GET OUT OF SWIMMING

1. Hide swimming things.

2. Cover face in green spots.

Unfortunately, his mum didn't fall for it...

You'll enjoy swimming when you get there.

"Come on," she said, taking Billy by the hand. "Your sister and I will be there cheering you on. It will all be fine."

21

Chapter 2
Into the Pool

Everyone else seemed really **excited** about the diving competition.

"I bet I do come last," thought Billy. **Meanwhile...**

...the Mini Monsters crept into Billy's locker to go over their plan.

"Quickly," said Captain Snott. "Remember the plan..."

MAKE BILLY BRILLIANT AT SWIMMING PLAN

1. Climb up to the highest diving board.

2. Get Billy to join us.

3. Help Billy to jump off the diving board.

4. Billy wins the diving competition with our help!

As soon as he got into the pool, Billy looked up at the diving boards. They were completely

TERRIFYING.

"We'll have our lesson first," said Mr. Roberts, the swimming teacher, "then it'll be time for the competition."

"And there's a race going on in the lanes," Mr. Roberts went on. "So whatever you do, keep to **this area** of the pool."

31

33

Chapter 3
Overboard!

Billy tried to listen to Mr. Roberts, but his eyes kept flicking towards the highest diving board.

Everytime he saw it, he got a **WORRIED** feeling in his tummy.

He wished
he had wings,
like Peep…

…or a cape,
like Captain
Snott…

…or **stretchy**
powers, like
Gloop.

"That's funny," thought Billy, looking across the pool, "I'm thinking about the Mini Monsters so much..."

...I can actually see them.

Billy rubbed his eyes and looked again. No, he realized, those *were* the Mini Monsters.

Billy was staring at them so hard he forgot to swim.

CRASH!

Then, to Billy's horror, a huge wave came… and knocked the Mini Monsters overboard.

One moment they were
on the floats…
the next,
they were

GONE!

Billy swam faster than he ever had before – straight through one racing lane…

Oops!

Sorry!

…and then another.

Mr. Roberts was looking furious. And amazed.

But Billy didn't have time to stop.

I never knew the boy could swim like that!

"Got you!" said Billy, snatching the Mini Monsters out of the water.

Captain Snott looked around.

"**Oh no!**" he cried. "Where's Gloop?"

That's when the Mini Monsters saw Gloop. He was at the bottom of the pool being sucked down the drain!

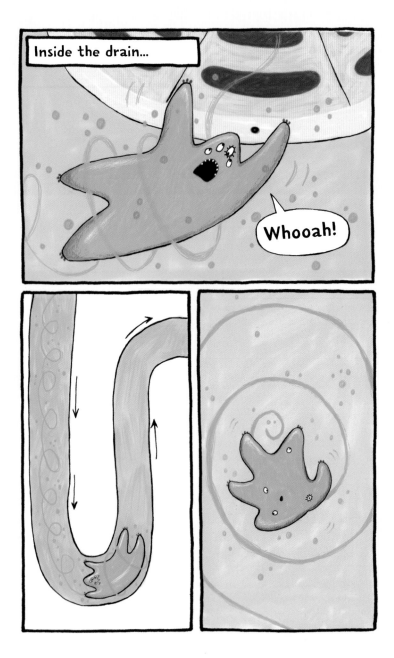

42

Chapter 4
The Competition

Mr. Roberts came storming over. "What were you doing, Billy?"

"We'll have to talk about it later," his swimming teacher went on.

The competition is about to start.

Billy followed Mr. Roberts to the diving pool.

He joined the other children on the benches. He could see his mum waving at him.

One by one,

all the other
boys and girls

jumped off
the boards.

Even the best, bravest swimmers
didn't make it to the top one.

At last it was Billy's turn. "I'll just hold my nose and shut my eyes," he told himself.

But as he walked past the high board he looked up. To his **HORROR**, there were the Mini Monsters. Climbing up the ladder.

There were gasps from the crowd as Billy stepped out onto the highest board.

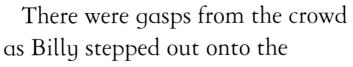

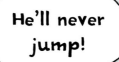
That's Billy!

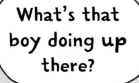
What's that boy doing up there?

He'll never jump!

Billy reached down to pick up the
Mini Monsters. But Gloop had left
a trail of slime behind him.
Billy slipped…

Whoooah!

…and wobbled…

…and slid right
to the end of the
diving board.

Aaargh!

For a moment, he stood looking
down at the water. It
seemed
very
far
away.

Billy could hear cheers from the Mini Monsters behind him.

You can do it, Billy!

We're right behind you!

Are we?

Billy shut his eyes, took a deep breath, and jumped...

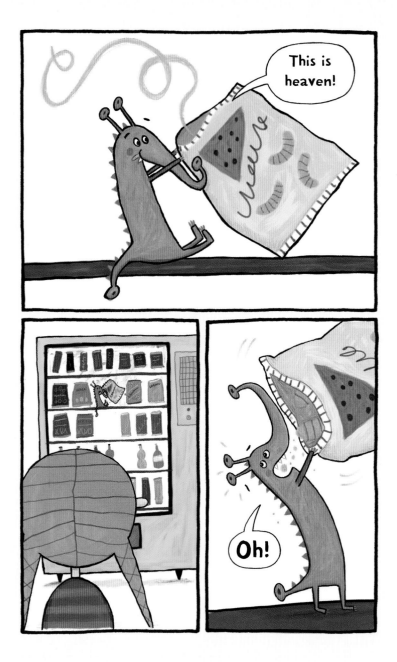

60

Chapter 5
Champion!

Billy landed in the water
with a **SPLASH!**

He could hear tiny splashes
as the Mini Monsters landed
beside him.

I really
did it!

I did it!

Mr. Roberts came rushing over.
"Billy! How amazing! You've won
first prize!"

Billy couldn't believe it either.

He stood on the top of the podium and was given a gold medal and a trophy.

Back in the changing rooms, the
Mini Monsters were celebrating, too.

"But where's Trumpet? And Peep?"
asked Billy.

"Trumpet went to find some
cheese," said Captain Snott. "And
Peep went after him."

We all
dived off
the board!

I want to
do it again!

After Billy had got changed, everyone wanted to congratulate him.

But Billy was busy trying to work out where Peep and Trumpet could have gone...

"I'd like to buy you a treat," said his mum, "for doing so well. Shall we go to a cafe? What would you like?"

"That's it!" Billy realized suddenly. "The snack machine!"

Trumpet was always near food. He had to be *inside* the snack machine. Especially if it sold anything with CHEESE in it.

By the snack machine...

I know those legs!

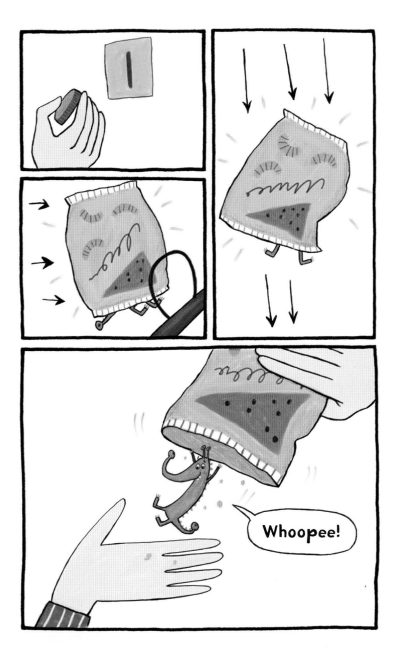

Chapter 6
Monster Gala

"Well done," said Billy's mum, on the way home. "I was so proud of you."

I knew you could do it. You're a swimming star.

As soon as Billy got home, he rushed up to his room.

"That was amazing!" he said, looking at the Mini Monsters.

Let's celebrate...

"...with a swimming gala of our own!"

All about the
MINI MONSTERS

FANG-FACE →

LIKES EATING:
socks, school ties,
paper, or anything
that comes his way.

SPECIAL SKILL:
has massive fangs.

SCARE FACTOR:
9/10

← GLOOP

LIKES EATING: cake.

SPECIAL SKILL:
very stre-e-e-e-tchy.
Gloop can also swallow
his own eyeballs and
make them reappear on
any part of his body.

SCARE FACTOR:
4/10

CAPTAIN SNOTT →

LIKES EATING: bogeys.

SPECIAL SKILL:
can glow in the dark.

**SCARE
FACTOR:
5/10**

PEEP

LIKES EATING: very small flies.

SPECIAL SKILL: can fly (but
not very far, or very well).

**SCARE FACTOR:
0/10** (unless you're afraid of
small hairy things)

TRUMPET →

LIKES EATING: cheese.

SPECIAL SKILL:
amazingly powerful
cheese-powered parps.

**SCARE FACTOR:
7/10**
(taking into
account his parps)

Edited by Lesley Sims and Becky Walker
Designed by Brenda Cole
Cover design by Hannah Cobley

Digital Manipulation by John Russell

First published in 2017 by Usborne Publishing Ltd., Usborne House,
83-85 Saffron Hill, London EC1N 8RT, England. www.usborne.com
Copyright © 2017 Usborne Publishing Ltd. UKE

Collect all the **MINI MONSTERS** adventures!